City BEET

Written by
TZIPORAH COHEN

Illustrated by
UDAYANA LUGO

PUBLISHED BY SLEEPING BEAR PRESS™

"Raw beet and garlic salad?"
said Victoria to Mrs. Kosta.

SIGN-UP

SAVE the DATE!
POTLUCK
BLOCK
PARTY

JULY 16th

DAY
CARE

YOU SEEN
PARKY?

OGA

They marched down to the corner store to buy the seed.

When they got home, they dug.

Between April showers, they planted.

In May, while the birds twittered, they watered and fertilized.

Under the warm June sun,
they weeded and mulched and sang.

And they watched their beet grow.

And grow.

And grOW.

On potluck day, Mrs. Kosta woke Victoria up early. "Time to harvest!"

Victoria watched while Mrs. Kosta pulled with all her might.

But that big red beet wouldn't budge.

BEEP, BEEP!

Mr. Wen drove up in his newly washed taxi. "Need some help?"

Victoria read the recipe while Mr. Wen
tugged and tugged at Mrs. Kosta,

who hooked her arms around that big
red beet and pulled with all her might.

But that big red beet wouldn't budge.

Not even
ONE
LITTLE
BIT.

Victoria came over to help,
but Mr. Wen shook his head.
"You're too small," he said.

BWEEP BIP BWEEP!

Officers Deena and Tina pulled up in their cruiser. "Heard there was some trouble on the block."

Victoria minced the garlic while
Officers Deena and Tina tugged
and tugged at Mr. Wen,

who tugged
at Mrs. Kosta,

who held tight to that big red beet
and pulled with all her might.

But that big red beet wouldn't budge.

Not even ONE LITTLE BIT.

Victoria got in line to tug. Officers Deena and Tina grunted, "You'll have to grow a bit first."

SWISH, SWISH!

Mr. Vitelli jumped out of his street sweeper. "Ciao! Need another hand?"

Victoria mixed the olive oil and balsamic vinegar as Mr. Vitelli tugged and tugged at Officers Deena and Tina,

who tugged at Mr. Wen,

who tugged
at Mrs. Kosta,

who grabbed that big red beet
and pulled with all her might.

But that big red beet
wouldn't budge.

Not even

ONE
LITTLE
BIT.

Victoria tried again to help. "We've got this," said Mr. Vitelli with a wink.

"Super City Recycling at your service!" said
Mr. Azizi with a bow. "May I be of assistance?"

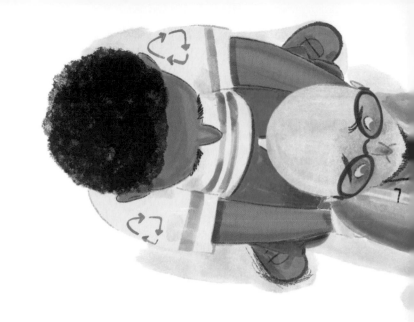

Victoria chopped the parsley and sprinkled the salt and pepper while

Mr. Azizi tugged and tugged at Mr. Vitelli,

who tugged at Officers Deena and Tina,

who tugged
at Mr. Wen,

who tugged
at Mrs. Kosta,

who gripped that big red beet
and pulled with all her might.

But that big red beet wouldn't budge.

Not even ONE
LITTLE
BIT.

Victoria studied the situation.

SQUEAL!

41

Ms. Browne parked the
Number 41. "You're blocking
the bus lane, folks!"

Victoria headed across the street as Ms. Browne tugged and tugged at Mr. Azizi, who tugged at Mr. Vitelli, who tugged at Officers Deena and Tina, who tugged at Mr. Wen, who tugged at Mrs. Kosta, who grasped that big red beet and pulled with all her might.

But that big red beet
wouldn't budge.

Not even
ONE
LITTLE
BIT.

RING, ring! RING, ring!

who tugged
at Mr. Vitelli,

who tugged
at Mr. Azizi,

Victoria pedaled as
hard as she could,
tugging at Ms. Browne,

who tugged
at Mrs. Kosta,

who tugged
at Mr. Wen,

who tugged at Officers
Deena and Tina,

who clutched that big red beet
with her last ounce of strength.

And that
BIG RED
CITY BEET?

Mrs. Kosta grabbed her grater.

Just in time, too.

AUTHOR'S NOTE

I've lived in lots of places, and in each place I end up, it's important to me to find other people to talk to and share experiences with. People aren't meant to be alone, and communities make us feel less lonely, support us when we need help, and even make us healthier! Each person in a community has something to give, and even the smallest bit helps. When we work together, we can accomplish big things. Even in a large city, we can find a small community of people to spend time with, rely on for help, or share a good meal with. Who lives in your community? How can you help people in your community get to know one another better? Maybe you can even start a community garden and grow your favorite vegetables!

"Butternut squash pie?"
said Victoria to Mrs. Kosta.

SAVE THE DATE

COMMUNIT
THANKSGIVIN
DINNER

NOVEMBER 26

Raw Beet & Garlic Salad

1 pound raw beets, grated

1 large garlic clove, minced

1 tablespoon finely chopped fresh parsley

1 tablespoon extra-virgin olive oil

2 tablespoons balsamic vinegar

1/4 teaspoon sea salt

1/8 teaspoon freshly ground pepper

Combine all ingredients in bowl and stir to mix.

For Asher and Eyla
And for all the essential workers, everywhere
—Tziporah

For my mom, who makes a killer beet salad, and
for my cousin Claudia, who can't have enough of it
—UL

SLEEPING BEAR PRESS™

2395 South Huron Parkway, Suite 200
Ann Arbor, MI 48104
www.sleepingbearpress.com

Printed and bound in the United States.

10 9 8 7 6 5 4 3 2 1

Library of Congress Cataloging-in-Publication Data on file.

ISBN 9781534112711